MY ONE AND ONL

TOTTENHAM
HOTSPUR

THE OFFICIAL
TOTTENHAM
HOTSPUR
ANNUAL 2025

Written by Andy Greeves & Cathryn Greeves

Designed by Dan Brawn

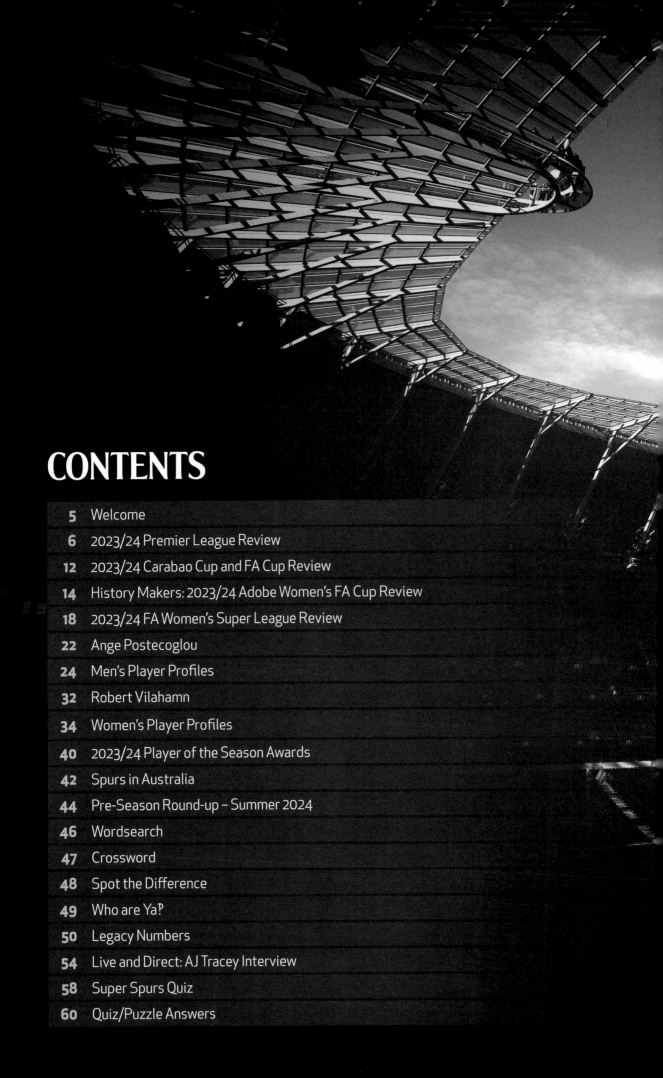

CONTENTS

WELCOME TO THE OFFICIAL TOTTENHAM HOTSPUR ANNUAL 2025

On the back of promising debut campaigns for Men's Head Coach Ange Postecoglou and Women's Head Coach Robert Vilahamn, the calendar year of 2025 promises to be another exciting one for Tottenham Hotspur.

Ange guided our Men's team to a fifth-place finish in the Premier League in 2023/24, securing a return to European football in the UEFA Europa League. Vilahamn's Women's side meanwhile reached the Adobe Women's FA Cup Final and also secured their first-ever FA Women's Super League victory over local rivals Arsenal during the campaign.

This Annual profiles the players who make our respective teams tick, from top goalkeepers like Becky Spencer and Guglielmo Vicario through to electric forwards such as Heung-Min Son and Bethany England.

Elsewhere in this Annual, we hear from lifelong Spurs fan and music star AJ Tracey while we learn more about the legacy numbers that appear on the back of our Men's first team shirts. There are also puzzles to solve and a Super Spurs Quiz to test your knowledge of your favourite club and plenty more besides.

Enjoy your new Annual and COME ON YOU SPURS!

#COYS

Andy Greeves

2023/24 PREMIER LEAGUE REVIEW

We finished fifth in the Premier League table in 2023/24 with 20 wins and six draws, securing qualification for the UEFA Europa League in 2024/25.

We made our best-ever start to a Premier League campaign as we took 26 points from our opening 10 games with important wins over Manchester United and Liverpool and a hard-fought draw at Arsenal during that period.

Newly-appointed Club captain Heung-Min Son registered his 300th Premier League appearance as we took on Liverpool at Anfield on May 5, 2024 – a game in which he also netted his 120th league goal in Lilywhite colours.

AUGUST

We opened our Premier League campaign under new boss Ange Postecoglou with an entertaining 2-2 draw at Brentford. All four goals were scored in the first half, with Cristian Romero and Emerson Royal netting for Spurs.

Next up was a visit from Manchester United, who we sent home empty-handed. In a game of many chances which saw both sides hit the woodwork, Pape Matar Sarr finally broke the deadlock four minutes after the break and an own-goal from Lisandro Martinez sealed our well-deserved victory late on.

Our unbeaten run continued on the south coast as new signing James Maddison scored his first Spurs goal from Sarr's perfect through ball against AFC Bournemouth. Destiny Udogie did all the hard work for our second, setting up Dejan Kulusevski who netted from close range.

Our fantastic performances in August earnt Ange the Premier League Manager of the Month Award.

SEPTEMBER

Despite going behind after just four minutes at Burnley, we fought back to win 5-2 at Turf Moor. Sonny scored a hat-trick - his fourth in the Premier League - while Romero and Maddison also bagged their second league goals of the season in the victory.

We had to come from behind to beat newly-promoted Sheffield United too – and what an incredible turnaround it was! With 97 minutes on the clock, we were still trailing 1-0 at Tottenham Hotspur Stadium, but substitute Richarlison headed home Ivan Perišić's corner before then picking out Kulusevski two minutes later, who fired home our winner.

A Sonny brace earnt us a point in the north London derby at the Emirates. The Gunners took the lead on 26 minutes when Romero deflected the ball into his own net but our captain pulled us level just before the break. Arsenal went in front again from the penalty spot after Romero handballed but Maddison played Son in for his second of the day on 55 minutes.

We ended the month with a dramatic 2-1 home victory over nine-man Liverpool. We went ahead after 36 minutes of the match as Sonny got on the end of a pass from Richarlison. The Reds equalised on the stroke of half-time before Joel Matip scored an own goal with just seconds left on the clock to give us the win.

OCTOBER

Our unbeaten run in the league continued into October as Micky van de Ven scored the only goal against Premier League debutants Luton Town at Kenilworth Road to send us to the top of the table. The centre-back got onto the end of a Maddison corner to net his first goal for Spurs after we went down to 10 men when Yves Bissouma received his second yellow card of the afternoon.

We returned to pole position at the end of match week 10 with a 2-0 home victory over Fulham. Sonny got our first with a curling effort before Maddison sealed victory with an almost carbon copy strike on 54 minutes.

Our 2-1 defeat of Crystal Palace at the end of October saw us move five points clear at the top of the Premier League table. Joel Ward turned the ball into his own net for our opener and Sonny doubled our lead midway through the second half when he struck home from a Brennan Johnson cutback. The Eagles netted four minutes into injury time but it proved only a consolation.

NOVEMBER

It wasn't until early November that we endured our first Premier League defeat of the season at the hands of former boss Mauricio Pochettino's Chelsea. Kulusevski scored after just seven minutes and Sonny thought he had doubled our advantage soon after but it was ruled out for offside. Chelsea had two efforts also disallowed by VAR before Romero was sent off and Cole Palmer converted from the spot to make it 1-1 just after the half-hour mark of this frenetic encounter. We went down to nine men when Udogie received his second booking and though we continued to create further chances, a Nicolas Jackson hat-trick saw the Blues take all three points.

Despite taking early leads in our next two Premier League games – through Brennan Johnson at Wolverhampton Wanderers and from Giovani Lo Celso against Aston Villa – we suffered 2-1 defeats on both occasions as November proved a month to forget.

DECEMBER

There was late drama at the Etihad Stadium as a 90th-minute header from Kulusevski saw us snatch a point in a six goal-thriller against the Premier League champions, Manchester City. We went in front through Son on six minutes only for our captain to deflect the ball into his own net three minutes later. The hosts led 2-1 at the break but Lo Celso levelled for Spurs from the edge of the area midway through the second half. Jack Grealish thought he had sealed victory for City with nine minutes to play but Kulusevski headed home in stoppage time to give us a deserved share of the spoils.

After a 2-1 loss against West Ham United in N17 – with Romero on target for Spurs – we got back to winning ways with a comprehensive 4-1 home victory over Newcastle United three days later. Udogie put us ahead before Richarlison added a goal either side of the break and captain Son completed our rout from the penalty spot on 85 minutes.

Goals from Richarlison and Kulusevski saw us pick up all three points at Nottingham Forest and we made it three wins in three as we beat Everton 2-1 at Tottenham Hotspur Stadium two days before Christmas. Our number 9 was on target once again against his former club with Son netting our second after Everton goalkeeper Jordan Pickford palmed away an initial powerful shot from Johnson.

Alejo Véliz and Ben Davies scored late on in a 4-2 defeat to Brighton & Hove Albion in our sixth game of December but we finished 2023 on a high by beating AFC Bournemouth 3-1 on New Year's Eve thanks to strikes from Sarr, Son and Richarlison.

JANUARY

Our first game of 2024 saw us come from behind twice to draw 2-2 at Manchester United. Richarlison netted his sixth goal in as many Premier League games to cancel out Rasmus Højlund's opener and after Marcus Rashford put United back in front, Bentancur hit a screamer just after the restart to pull us level once more.

Our only other league match in January saw us complete a season 'double' over Brentford. Udogie, Johnson and Richarlison scored within the space of eight second-half minutes to give us a 3-2 victory.

A brace from Richarlison saw us draw 2-2 at Everton at the beginning of February which was followed by a 2-1 home win against Brighton. It was looking like both teams would have to settle for a point after Pascal Groß converted from the penalty spot for the Seagulls and Sarr equalised with his second attempt after the first hit the post just after the hour mark. But Johnson scored a last-gasp winner after being set up by Son, who was making his first Spurs appearance since returning from the Asian Cup with South Korea.

Wolves beat us 2-1 courtesy of a João Gomes brace in our final game of the month, with Kulusevski getting our goal in the first minute of the second half.

MARCH

Three goals in 11 minutes saw us complete an impressive comeback against Crystal Palace at Tottenham Hotspur Stadium. Timo Werner – on loan from RB Leipzig – netted his first Spurs goal to pull us level on 77 minutes before Romero headed home a Maddison cross and Son completed the fightback with two minutes of the 90 remaining.

We pulled off a huge 4-0 victory over 10-man Aston Villa in the race for a top-four finish. After a goalless first half, Maddison opened the scoring when he slid home a square ball from Sarr. Just three minutes later Johnson doubled our lead, and after Villa captain John McGinn was sent off for his challenge on Udogie we added a further two through Son and Werner.

A 3-0 London derby defeat at Fulham preceded a 2-1 victory over Luton Town where an own goal from the Hatters' Issa Kaboré pulled us level on 51 minutes before Son bagged all three points late on.

APRIL

Our trip to the London Stadium to take on West Ham United finished in a 1-1 draw. Johnson's fifth-minute strike was cancelled out by a header from West Ham's Kurt Zouma, and though we pushed for a winner late on we weren't able to make the breakthrough.

Second-half strikes from Van de Ven and Pedro Porro ensured we picked up another three points against Nottingham Forest at Tottenham Hotspur Stadium. Murillo put Werner's cross into his own net for our opener before Chris Wood levelled for the visitors. Fine goals from two of our defenders wrapped up the win - our sixth consecutive Premier League victory over Forest.

Our other two games in April - against Newcastle and Arsenal - ended in disappointing defeats.

MAY

After two difficult games against Chelsea (0-2) and Liverpool (2-4) - where there was a personal highlight for captain Son who reached his 300 Premier League games milestone at Anfield - we beat Burnley 2-1 at home. The Clarets took the lead through Jacob Bruun Larsen but Porro smashed in our equaliser with half an hour on the clock and Van de Ven made certain of all three points when he slotted the ball into the bottom corner late on.

Erling Haaland was on fine form as Manchester City beat us 2-0 en route to their fourth consecutive Premier League title before we ended the 2023/24 season in style with an enjoyable 3-0 win at Sheffield United on the final day of the campaign. Kulusevski broke the deadlock on 14 minutes after being set up by Son, and Porro fired home a first-time effort just before the hour mark to double our lead. Our number 21 then bagged his brace to secure us a fifth place Premier League finish and UEFA Europa League qualification for 2024/25.

REVIEW

In 2023/24, we reached the fourth round of the Emirates FA Cup and the second round of the Carabao Cup.

CARABAO CUP

Second Round
Fulham 1-1 Spurs
(Spurs won 5-3 on penalties)

Our Carabao Cup campaign in 2023/24 began and ended at Craven Cottage. A Micky van de Ven own goal gave Fulham the lead on 19 minutes, but Spurs were livelier in the second half. Our efforts paid off as a fine cross from Ivan Perišić found Richarlison, who headed home his first goal of the season to level the scores on 56 minutes - the Whites only had 10 men on the pitch at the time as Kenny Tete had to run off to change his boot.

Our recent signing Manor Solomon came close against his former side late on as we went in search of the winner, but the tie went to penalties and Fulham netted all five to progress.

EMIRATES FA CUP

Third Round
Spurs 1-0 Burnley

We kicked off our FA Cup campaign in the third round against fellow Premier League side Burnley. It was a relatively quiet first half in north London with Richarlison, Brennan Johnson and Giovani Lo Celso all missing opportunities to score.

Pedro Porro finally broke the deadlock for Spurs in the 78th minute with a superb strike from 25 yards out after winning back possession.

The Clarets twice brought 'keeper Arijanet Muric up for corners late on as they tried to find an equaliser, but Spurs - without captain Heung-Min Son, Pape Matar Sarr and Yves Bissouma, who were away on international duty with their respective countries - held on to progress to round four.

Fourth Round
Spurs 0-1 Manchester City

Manchester City finally scored their first goal at Tottenham Hotspur Stadium after five successive defeats in all competitions at Spurs' new home without netting.

Our excellent defence kept Pep Guardiola's side at bay for 88 minutes of the fourth-round match before Nathan Aké tapped in from close range during a goalmouth scramble to give City victory and a place in the fifth round.

The game did see the return of James Maddison - who came on as a substitute after three months out with an ankle injury against that season's FA Cup runners-up.

HISTORY MAKERS!
SPURS ARE ON THEIR WAY TO WEMBLEY!

A memorable and historic season in the Adobe Women's FA Cup in 2023/24 saw us reach the final of the competition for the first time. Spurs Women beat the likes of Manchester City and Leicester City en route to the showpiece occasion against Manchester United at Wembley Stadium.

FOURTH ROUND
Spurs 3-2 Sheffield United

Spurs fought back from 2-0 down to win 3-2 against Sheffield United in the fourth round of the FA Cup. Sophie Haywood and Jessica Sigsworth netted for the Blades before Tottenham captain Bethany England struck twice within 11 minutes – the second from the penalty spot after Tara Bourne brought down Jessica Naz – to bring us level with just 10 minutes of the 90 remaining. As the seconds ticked by, it looked like a replay was inevitable, but in the sixth minute of added time Rosella Ayane completed our dramatic comeback with a composed finish from a brilliant diagonal ball from Olga Ahtinen .

FIFTH ROUND
Spurs 1-0 Charlton Athletic

Kit Graham scored the only goal of the match against her former side as we saw off Charlton Athletic in the fifth round. The forward, who netted more than 200 times during her 14 years with the Addicks, came off the substitutes bench to score in the 76th minute. Amy James-Turner played the ball in to Graham, who initially lost possession before it was gifted back to her by Charlton's Melissa Johnson, and she drove it home from distance with her left foot.

QUARTER-FINAL Spurs 1-1 Manchester City (AET – Spurs won 4-3 on penalties)

A goal from England deep in injury time forced our quarter-final tie with Manchester City into extra time. Mary Fowler opened the scoring for City after just six minutes at Brisbane Road when her effort took a big deflection off James-Turner and ended up in the back of the net. Naz had opportunities to equalise but was unable to find the target and City looked resolute. But, in the sixth minute of injury time, our captain capitalised on a defensive mix-up and slotted the ball into City's empty net to make it 1-1. Both sides pushed for a winner in extra time, Chloe Kelly came closest when her free-kick rattled the crossbar, but the game went to penalties.

Spurs 'keeper Becky Spencer proved the hero, saving City's first two spot-kicks from Alex Greenwood and Kelly, and after England, Amanda Nildén and Shuang Wang all converted, it was left to James-Turner to secure Spurs' place in the last four of the competition for the first time ever – and she didn't disappoint.

SEMI-FINAL Spurs 2-1 Leicester City (AET)

Our women came from behind once again to see off Leicester City in an exciting FA Cup semi-final in front of 18,000 supporters at Tottenham Hotspur Stadium. The Foxes took an early lead through Jutta Rantala but we never stopped pushing for an equaliser and Naz finally found the net in the 83rd minute to force extra-time. Despite chances for both teams in extra-time it looked like the game was going all the way to penalties again – but Martha Thomas, returning from a hamstring injury, had other ideas. In the 118th minute, our number 17 rose highest after Luana Bühler flicked on Matilda Vinberg's ball, and she headed over Lize Kop in Leicester's goal to write her name in the history books, and secure our place at Wembley.

FINAL
Manchester United 4-0 Spurs

There was heartbreak at the final hurdle for Spurs Women as we finished our FA Cup journey as runners-up to Manchester United. Robert Vilahamn's side held their own during the first half at Wembley with Matilda Vinberg having a couple of decent chances, but England international Ella Toone broke the deadlock for United with a superb strike from 22 yards out on the stroke of half-time.

Former Spur Rachel Williams doubled their advantage early in the second half and just three minutes later Lucia Garcia netted a third. England came within inches of pulling a goal back for Spurs just after the hour mark but her header hit the crossbar, and Garcia bagged her brace late on to secure United the trophy in front of a crowd of 76,000.

TIME
TO
RISE

SPURS ⚽ SHOP

2024/25 HOME KIT

Scan me

REVIEW

OCTOBER

Our campaign kicked off with a trip to last season's WSL winners, Chelsea. New signing Martha Thomas netted her first goal in our colours in a spirited performance but it finished 2-1 to the hosts at Stamford Bridge.

A week later we recorded our first league win of the campaign with Olga Ahtinen, Thomas and Eveliina Summanen on target in a 3-1 victory over newly-promoted Bristol City at Brisbane Road – our main home venue once again in 2023/24. Our winning run continued with a triumph at Brighton & Hove Albion where the Seagulls' opener was cancelled out by Thomas on the stroke of half-time, before Manchester United loanee Grace Clinton and Ria Percival made it 3-1 to Spurs.

Scotland international Thomas was on fire once again in our last game of the month against Aston Vila as she bagged a hat-trick – the club's first-ever in the WSL. Ashleigh Neville also netted in the 4-2 victory in Walsall, to send us to the top of the league table.

Thomas' incredible start to life in N17 saw her named WSL Player of the Month for October.

2023/24 was Spurs Women's fifth consecutive season in the Barclays FA Women's Super League (WSL). We finished sixth in the table on 31 points, with eight wins, seven draws and seven defeats – just one point off our record points tally in the top flight.

The biggest WSL highlight was beating Arsenal 1-0 at Tottenham Hotspur Stadium – our first league victory over our local rivals. We also picked up points against Manchester United and Liverpool – who both finished in the top five.

Martha Thomas – who scored the winner against Arsenal in December 2023 – topped our WSL goalscoring charts with seven strikes, and 10 in all competitions.

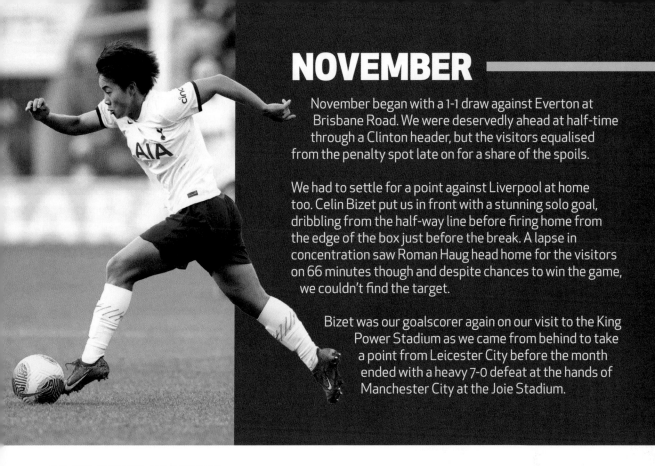

NOVEMBER

November began with a 1-1 draw against Everton at Brisbane Road. We were deservedly ahead at half-time through a Clinton header, but the visitors equalised from the penalty spot late on for a share of the spoils.

We had to settle for a point against Liverpool at home too. Celin Bizet put us in front with a stunning solo goal, dribbling from the half-way line before firing home from the edge of the box just before the break. A lapse in concentration saw Roman Haug head home for the visitors on 66 minutes though and despite chances to win the game, we couldn't find the target.

Bizet was our goalscorer again on our visit to the King Power Stadium as we came from behind to take a point from Leicester City before the month ended with a heavy 7-0 defeat at the hands of Manchester City at the Joie Stadium.

DECEMBER

Captain Bethany England returned from a hip injury for the Manchester United visit in early December but despite controlling the early part of the game, we went down to a 4-0 defeat. Our second game of the month saw us make history with our first-ever win over Arsenal in front of almost 20,000 fans at Tottenham Hotspur Stadium.

Thomas opened the scoring early in the second half as she slid home Bizet's pass, and we defended superbly for the remainder of the game with goalkeeper Barbora Votíková in excellent form on her first WSL start.

As well as it being a memorable day on the pitch for the team, there was a personal achievement for England too as our captain recorded her 150th appearance in the WSL.

JANUARY

Our first WSL fixture of 2024 proved to be an exciting seven-goal thriller as we edged out West Ham United 4-3 at Victoria Road. Clinton opened the scoring for Spurs after just six minutes with a low drive into the bottom corner before Risa Shimizu grabbed the equaliser just after the half-hour mark. Bizet put us back in front shortly before the break and Clinton bagged her brace three minutes into the second half with a first-time effort to extend our advantage. The Hammers scored twice within eight minutes to pull level before Jess Naz sealed victory with a shot into the bottom right corner on 75 minutes.

Manchester City were the visitors to Brisbane Road for our other WSL game in January. New signing Amanda Nildén was handed her first WSL start but despite a gutsy performance from Spurs, an own goal from Amy James-Turner and a strike from Khadija Shaw saw City take home all three points.

FEBRUARY

Liverpool scored a stoppage-time equaliser to deny us all three points at Prenton Park at the beginning of February. We went in front through Bizet 19 minutes from time and worked hard to see out the game, but Marie Hobinger fired home for the Reds in the first minute of added time to make it 1-1.

Aston Villa got revenge for our October triumph over them, as they ran out 2-1 winners at Brisbane Road. James-Turner headed home from Summanen's free-kick for her first WSL goal to level the score on 38 minutes, following Adriana Leon's opener for Villa. We upped our game in the second half but Villa restored their lead on the hour mark through Jordan Nobbs and we were unable to find another equaliser.

MARCH

We were unable to complete the double over our north London rivals in March, as Arsenal claimed a narrow 1-0 victory at the Emirates. Naz came closest for Spurs as her effort was tipped onto the crossbar by Manuela Zinsberger in the first half before Alessia Russo delivered the sucker punch four minutes after the break, firing home from close range.

We returned to winning ways in the WSL with a 1-0 victory over Leicester City. After being handed her first league start, Matilda Vinberg scored from a Naz cross just two minutes into the match at Brisbane Road. Drew Spence should have doubled our advantage but her effort struck the woodwork and Becky Spencer made a fantastic double save shortly before half-time. We had further chances in the closing stages with Kit Graham seeing her shot cleared off the line and England had the ball in the back of the net, only for it to be disallowed for being offside.

It also took just two minutes of our match at Ashton Gate to go in front a week later as England netted her first WSL goal of the campaign with a low, left-foot shot against Bristol City. The Robins pushed hard for an equaliser, but we held on to record back-to-back clean sheets in the league.

APRIL

An-injury time strike from Maya Le Tissier denied Spurs all three points from their hard-fought encounter with Manchester United at Leigh Sports Village.

The hosts went ahead on 13 minutes but two goals in as many minutes from England and Naz saw us take the lead around the half-hour mark. Robert Vilahamn's side defended resolutely, producing some last-ditch tackles and Becky Spencer was in inspiring form in the Spurs goal, but United grabbed the equaliser late on to make it 2-2.

England's third WSL goal in as many games ensured we took a point from our clash with Brighton at the end of April. The Seagulls went ahead in the 17th minute through Elisabeth Terland but our captain guided home Ashleigh Neville's cross with just nine minutes left on the clock to pull us level.

MAY

Spence and England were on target as we came from 2-0 down to draw with Everton at Walton Hall Park. The hosts netted twice within the first 15 minutes of our final away game of the season, giving us a steep hill to climb. But Spurs showed character and Spence latched onto a superb ball from Summanen to fire into an empty net on the stroke of half-time to halve the deficit. Just minutes after the restart, England pulled us level as Spence won possession before playing a perfect ball for our number 9 to tap in.

Following a narrow 1-0 defeat to Chelsea at Brisbane Road we ended our WSL campaign on a high in front of 10,000 fans at Tottenham Hotspur Stadium. England's half-volley in the fourth minute opened the scoring against West Ham but the visitors pulled one back on 50 minutes. We never stopped pushing for a second, and substitute Naz finally found the net as she slotted home with four minutes of the 90 remaining. Spence rounded off the scoring with a wonderful strike from distance in the ninth minute of stoppage time to wrap up the three points.

FA WOMEN'S CONTINENTAL TYRES LEAGUE CUP (CONTI CUP) REVIEW 2023/24

A 6-0 thrashing of **Reading** saw our 2023/24 Conti Cup campaign get off to the perfect start. China international forward Zhang Linyan opened the scoring on her Spurs debut with Kit Graham, Asmita Ale, Ria Percival, Jessica Naz and Martha Thomas all getting on the scoresheet for the Group D clash too.

We followed that up with another victory in our second group game, this time seeing off **Bristol City** 3-0 thanks to goals from Graham, who netted from the penalty spot, and a brace from Rosella Ayane.

An exciting 3-3 draw with **Arsenal** went to penalties in December 2023 in our third group game. We took the lead three times through Thomas and two from Naz but Stina Blackstenius and Frida Maanum got the Gunners back level on two occasions before an unfortunate own goal from Amy Turner-James saw it finish 3-3, with a point for each side. Arsenal won the shootout 4-3 for an extra point to go top of the group.

A 3-0 victory over **Southampton** in our final group game saw us secure our place in the quarter-finals of the Conti Cup as Group D runners-up. Ramona Petzelberger, Charlotte Grant and Grace Clinton were Spurs' scorers at the Silverlake Stadium in Eastleigh.

Sadly, we didn't progress further than the final eight as we were narrowly beaten 1-0 by **Manchester City** at Brisbane Road on 7 February, 2024.

ANGE POSTECOGLOU

First Team Head Coach Ange Postecoglou won 20, drew six and lost 12 Premier League games during his debut season at Spurs, leading us to a fifth-place finish in the table and a spot in the UEFA Europa League in 2024/25.

Following his appointment on 6 June, 2023, Postecoglou recruited the likes of James Maddison, Micky van de Ven, Brennan Johnson and Guglielmo Vicario - who went on to enjoy excellent debut seasons in our colours.

A draw and two wins in his first three competitive matches saw Ange presented with the Premier League Manager of the Month award for August, 2023. We extended our unbeaten run in the league to 10 games, picking up 26 points in the process as we made our best-ever Premier League start under the Australian's guidance, as he also collected the monthly award for September and October. Another major accolade arrived in February, 2024 as he won the Manager of the Year prize at the London Football Awards.

In addition to putting points on the board, Postecoglou also won over our supporters in 2023/24 with his commitment to play attractive, attacking football. We netted 74 times in the Premier League during the season – our best goals return since 2017/18 when we also scored 74 times in the competition.

Born in Athens, Greece on 27 August, 1965, Ange grew up in Melbourne after moving to Australia as a five-year-old. He took up football, and as a defender he rose through the ranks at South Melbourne Hellas before going on to make 193 appearances for their first team between 1984 and 1993 and winning two championship titles during that time.

The left-back earned four caps for the Australia national team too before a knee injury ended his playing career and he moved into management. His first appointment was at South Melbourne in 1996 where he won two league titles before taking up a coaching position with the Australia national team's youth sides – a role he remained in for seven years.

After successful spells with Brisbane Roar and Melbourne Victory in the A-League, Postecoglou was appointed Australia senior national team manager in 2013. During his four years in charge, he led them to the 2014 FIFA World Cup and won the AFC Asian Cup in 2015.

In 2019, Ange also won Japan's J1 League with Yokohama F. Marinos prior to joining Celtic in 2021. The Australian had a hugely successful two seasons at Celtic Park, winning five major trophies - back-to-back Scottish Premiership titles and Scottish League Cups, and the Scottish Cup.

In his 27 years (and counting) as a coach, Ange has built teams with an aggressive and assertive style of play who dominate in possession. He certainly epitomises our motto: "To dare is to do".

MEN'S PLAYER PROFILES 2024/25

GUGLIELMO VICARIO

Known to his teammates simply as 'Vic', Guglielmo was ever-present for Spurs in the Premier League during an impressive debut campaign in N17. The Udine-born goalkeeper, who joined us from Serie A side Empoli in the summer of 2023, also played in both of our FA Cup matches to bring his appearances to 40 overall in 2023/24. Vic started his career at his local club Udinese and remained in the Italian leagues with the likes of Venezia and Cagliari before a loan move to Empoli became permanent in 2022. His performances between the sticks for Spurs earned him a first senior Italy cap in March, 2024, and he was also named Goalkeeper of the Year at the London Football Awards in the same month.

BRANDON AUSTIN

A product of the Spurs Academy, Brandon has been a regular member of our first team squad for the past two seasons. After being named as a substitute for the last 14 games of the 2023/24 campaign, the goalkeeper started in our post-season friendly against Newcastle United in Australia in May, 2024. That same month he signed a new contract with the Club which runs until 2029. Brandon has had two loan spells during his time at Spurs – at Viborg in Denmark in 2019/20 and Orlando City in the United States in 2021.

FRASER FORSTER

With Guglielmo Vicario in outstanding form, and then a couple of injuries including a fractured foot, Fraser made just one appearance for Spurs in 2023/24 to bring his games tally to 21 in all competitions since arriving from Southampton in July, 2022. The experienced stopper is a positive influence around Hotspur Way and was handed a new contract in December, 2023, that will keep him in N17 until the summer of 2025. An England international – who received his most recent call-up in March, 2023, but didn't feature – Fraser won multiple Scottish league and cup titles during his time with Celtic and has featured in the Champions League with both the Hoops, and Spurs in 2022/23.

PEDRO PORRO

An attack-minded full-back, Pedro is no stranger to scoring spectacular goals, such as his long-range effort to win us an Emirates FA Cup tie against Burnley in January, 2024. He also weighed in with three Premier League goals in 2023/24 as he made 37 appearances in all competitions. The former Manchester City and Sporting CP man, who joined us on loan for the second half of the 2022/23 season before making his move permanent in the summer of 2023, made his international debut for Spain in March, 2021.

CRISTIAN ROMERO

Cristian has been a model of consistency since signing for us from Atalanta, initially on loan in 2021 and then on a permanent deal in August 2022. The Argentine scored once in 30 appearances in all competitions for us in 2021/22 and followed that up with 34 appearances in both 2022/23 and 2023/24. The latter of those campaigns was his most productive in terms of goals, with Cristian netting against Brentford, Burnley, West Ham United, Crystal Palace and Arsenal. At international level, the defender has won both the FIFA World Cup and the Copa América.

BEN DAVIES

The 2024/25 season marks Ben's tenth campaign as a Spurs player, having signed for us from Swansea City in July 2014. The versatile defender, who can operate as a full-back or centre-back, had reached 330 Club appearances by the end of the 2023/24 season during which time he had also netted nine times. A regular for his country too, Ben is close to achieving a century of appearances for Wales while he appeared for them at both UEFA Euro 2016 and 2020 as well as the 2022 FIFA World Cup.

MICKY VAN DE VEN

There are fast footballers and then there's Micky van de Ven! Our Dutch defender was clocked at a mind-blowing top speed of 37.38 km/h (23.22mph) during our 3-2 victory over Brentford in January, 2024 – the highest speed by a player on record in England's top flight since records began in 2020. Having joined us from Bundesliga side VfL Wolfsburg in the summer of 2023, Micky enjoyed a wonderful debut season in our colours, scoring three times in 29 appearances in all competitions. He completed a clean sweep of the Club's Men's Player of the Season awards (see page 40 for more information) before heading to Germany to represent the Netherlands at UEFA Euro 2024.

DESTINY UDOGIE

The 2023/24 season marked a fine debut campaign in England's top flight for Destiny. After making his first appearance for us against Brentford on the opening weekend of the season, he went on to net twice in 30 matches in all competitions and was short listed for the Premier League's Young Player of the Season award. He also made his senior debut for Italy during the season, against Malta in October, 2023. Destiny originally joined us from Udinese in August, 2022 and was loaned back to the Serie A side for the 2022/23 season when he scored three times in 34 matches.

RADU DRAGUSIN

Along with Guglielmo Vicario (Italy), Micky van de Ven (Netherlands) and Pierre-Emile Højbjerg (Denmark), Radu was one of four Spurs players to be included in their national team squad for UEFA Euro 2024. He started all four of Romania's matches at the tournament, helping them top Group E before they were eliminated in the round of 16 by the Netherlands. Radu joined us from Italian side Genoa in January, 2024 and made his debut for us that month in a 2-2 Premier League draw at Manchester United – one of nine Club appearances through to the end of the campaign.

DJED SPENCE

Djed joined us from Middlesbrough in the summer of 2022 on the back of some impressive performances in the EFL Championship for both Boro and Nottingham Forest – for whom he was included in the PFA Championship Team of the Season during a loan spell there in 2021/22. Having helped Forest to promotion to the Premier League that season, he ironically made his Spurs debut at the City Ground as a substitute in a 2-0 win in August, 2022. Djed has spent time on loan at Rennes, Leeds United and Genoa since joining us.

YVES BISSOUMA

An energetic midfield performer, we swooped to sign Yves after four impressive seasons at Brighton & Hove Albion between 2018 and 2022, during which time he scored six goals in 124 appearances. The Mali international made his debut for us in our 4-1 win over Southampton on the opening weekend of the 2022/23 season. He made 28 appearances during that campaign and added a further 28 in 2023/24, as he started the season with consecutive Man of the Match performances against Brentford and Manchester United.

PAPE MATAR SARR

After featuring in 14 matches in his debut season with us in 2022/23, Pape became a regular feature of our midfield the following season, as he appeared in 34 of our 38 Premier League matches and also played in our Carabao Cup second round tie at Fulham. The Senegal international scored three goals during the campaign – all in home league victories over Manchester United, AFC Bournemouth and Brighton & Hove Albion. Pape originally signed for us from Metz in August, 2021 and was loaned back to the French club for the 2021/22 season.

ARCHIE GRAY

Aged 18 at the time, we signed midfielder Archie from Leeds United in July, 2024 on a six-year contract. He was part of the Gray footballing dynasty at Leeds – with Archie, his father Andy, grandfather Frank and great uncle Eddie all having played for the club. He made his Leeds debut on the opening weekend of the 2023/24 EFL Championship season – the first of 52 appearances in all competitions during the campaign as Leeds reached the play-off final at Wembley while Archie was named Championship Young Player of the Season.

RODRIGO BENTANCUR

Rodrigo made his first start of last season against Aston Villa in November, 2023 since sustaining a knee injury nine months earlier. Heartbreakingly, the player was on the wrong end of a poorly timed challenge in that game which resulted in an ankle injury and him missing the next six matches. Returning once again for our New Year's Eve 2023 clash against AFC Bournemouth, the Uruguayan was a regular in the second half of the season. His 24 outings during the campaign took his overall appearance tally to 68 in our colours, having joined us from Juventus halfway through the 2021/22 season.

LUCAS BERGVALL

Having reached an agreement to sign Lucas from Swedish Allsvenskan side Djurgarden back in February, 2024, the midfielder officially joined us in June, 2024 on a five-year-contract. Just 18 at the time, the Swede had already achieved so much in his short career. He made his senior competitive debut for IF Brommapojkarna (BP) in the Superettan (the second tier of Swedish football) aged 16 and featured 11 times as they gained promotion to the Allsvenskan in 2022. Lucas joined his brother, Theo, at Djurgarden for the 2023 and 2024 seasons before his move to N17.

DEJAN KULUSEVSKI

In his second full season with us, Dejan weighed in with eight goals in 39 appearances in 2023/24. The Sweden international originally joined us on an 18-month loan from Juventus midway through the 2021/22 season. His five goals in 18 Premier League games helped us on our way to a top four finish and UEFA Champions League qualification. The former Atalanta and Parma winger then netted twice in 37 appearances in his first full season in N17 in 2022/23, signing permanently for us in June, 2023.

NEW SIGNING

YANG MIN-HYEOK

In the summer of 2024, Yang put pen-to-paper on a deal to join the Club the following January from K League 1 side Gangwon FC. Spurs fans got a first glimpse of the South Korean when he lined up for Team K League as we beat them 4-3 in Seoul during pre-season. The winger progressed through the K League Under-18 Championship to become a first team regular at Gangwon, contributing eight goals and four assists during 2023/24. Internationally, Yang has represented his country at Under-16 and Under-17 levels and played in both the FIFA Under-17 World Cup and AFC Under-17 Asia Cup.

JAMES MADDISON

After a storming start to his Spurs career, which included three goals in his first 11 Premier League appearances for us, James suffered an injury against Chelsea in November 2023 that saw him ruled out for around three months. Our vice-captain returned to action in our Emirates FA Cup match against Manchester City in January 2024 and featured in 30 games for us in total by the end of the campaign. A huge Harry Potter fan, James played for Coventry City, Norwich City and Aberdeen (loan) before signing for us from Leicester City in June 2023.

BRENNAN JOHNSON

After a summer 2023 transfer deadline day move from Nottingham Forest, Wales international Brennan enjoyed an excellent first season in our colours in 2023/24. His debut came in our 2-1 victory over Sheffield United in September, 2023 while his five strikes in 34 matches included a dramatic late winner against Brighton & Hove Albion in February, 2024. He also made an impressive 10 Premier League assists during the season, which included set-ups for Timo Werner and Heung-Min Son's strikes in our 3-1 win over Crystal Palace in March 2024.

TIMO WERNER

Timo joined us on loan from RB Leipzig halfway through the 2023/24 season, with his debut coming in our 2-2 Premier League draw at Manchester United in January, 2024. His first Spurs goal came in our 3-1 home win over Crystal Palace in March, 2024 and a week later he netted in a 4-0 triumph at Aston Villa. Producing a number of eye-catching performances in his 14 appearances for us during the campaign, we reached an agreement with RB Leipzig in June, 2024 to loan the player again in 2024/25.

NEW SIGNING

WILSON ODOBERT

France Under-21 winger Wilson joined us from Burnley in August, 2024 after a single season with the Clarets that saw him score five goals in 34 appearances in all competitions. He began his career in the academy of Paris Saint-Germain before moving to Troyes in July, 2022, where he scored four goals in 32 appearances. Wilson, who has been capped by France at all levels between Under-16 and Under-21, was handed the number 28 shirt upon putting pen-to-paper on a four-year contract with us.

RICHARLISON

Richarlison marked his 50th Premier League appearance for Spurs with a late goal in our 2-1 victory over Sheffield United in September, 2023. After a short spell on the sidelines following groin surgery, the Brazil international returned with a fantastic goalscoring run, as he netted nine times in eight Premier League games up to and including our 2-2 draw with his former club Everton on 3 February, 2024. Richy left the Toffees to sign for us in July, 2022, and made 35 appearances in his debut season in N17. He also featured for Brazil at the 2022 FIFA World Cup in Qatar, scoring three goals which included a memorable scissor kick against Serbia in a 2-0 victory.

HEUNG-MIN SON

Sonny achieved another Spurs landmark during the 2023/24 season as his start in our 1-1 draw at West Ham United in April, 2024 was his 400th competitive appearance for us. Our Club captain became just the 14th player to reach that milestone in all competitions in our colours. This achievement came just three days after his 160th Club goal against Luton Town saw the South Korean overtake double-winning great Cliff Jones into fifth place on our list of top, all-time goalscorers behind Martin Chivers (174), Bobby Smith (208), Jimmy Greaves (266) and Harry Kane (280).

DOMINIC SOLANKE

Dominic signed for Spurs from AFC Bournemouth in August 2024 on the back of netting 19 goals for the south coast club during the previous campaign. The striker began his career with Chelsea where, upon making his first team debut in the UEFA Champions League in 2014, he became the Blues' youngest-ever player to feature in the competition. After a spell with Dutch side Vitesse Arnhem, Dominic signed for Liverpool in 2017 and then, 18 months later, made the move to the Cherries. He topped the Championship goalscoring charts in 2020/21 (jointly) and 2021/22 – where his 29 strikes helped Bournemouth win promotion back to the top flight. Dominic has featured for England across numerous youth levels and made his senior debut in November, 2017, in a friendly against Brazil at Wembley.

ROBERT VILAHAMN

Robert Vilahamn was appointed Spurs Women's Head Coach on 7 July, 2023 – and what a debut season it proved to be for the Swede. He led his side to an historic first-ever Adobe Women's FA Cup Final, and a sixth-place finish in the Barclays Women's Super League (WSL) in 2023/24, just one point short of our record tally in the top flight.

Born in Skalhamn, Sweden on 2 January, 1983 Vilahamn spent his entire professional playing career in his homeland, starting out at IFK Göteborg. The midfielder also featured for Bodens BK, FC Trollhättan, Qviding FIF and the Sweden Under-19s team, before signing for Kungälv-based side Ytterby IS in 2007. That was where he took his first steps into coaching in 2008, immediately leading the side to back-to-back promotions.

After a spell as head coach of the Under-19 team at Örgryte IS – during which time he set up his very own football academy in Uganda – Vilahamn then moved to Qviding FIF in 2018, winning promotion in both his seasons in charge. His next appointment was as assistant coach at tier one side BK Häcken, where he helped the men's team qualify for the inaugural UEFA Europa Conference League. Two years later he was given the top job with the club's women's team, securing UEFA Champions League qualification

in his first season and reaching the Swedish Cup Final in both 2022 and 2023.

Impressed with his track record, Spurs brought Vilahamn to north London hoping he could take our women's team to the next level – and bring silverware to the club. We came so close in 2023/24, finishing as runners-up to Manchester United in the Women's FA Cup following a 4-0 defeat in front of 76,000 fans at Wembley Stadium on 12 May, 2024.

We also reached the quarter-finals of the FA Women's League Cup before bowing out to Manchester City, and in the WSL, Vilahamn's side won eight of their 22 games in 2023/24, including a 1-0 victory over north London rivals Arsenal at Tottenham Hotspur Stadium on 16 December, 2023 – a feat never accomplished before. Mirroring Ange Postecoglou's approach with our men's first team, Vilahamn has changed the mentality of the women's side by inspiring confidence and allowing the team to play with freedom.

Following the final game of the campaign – a 3-1 London derby win over West Ham United – Vilahamn promised; "We will work really hard to be even better next season because this is just beginning."

> " WE WILL WORK REALLY HARD TO BE EVEN BETTER NEXT SEASON BECAUSE THIS IS JUST BEGINNING. "

WOMEN'S PLAYER PROFILES 2024/25

Profiles correct at the time of print.

BECKY SPENCER

Becky produced two stunning saves in our FA Cup quarter-final shootout against Manchester City in March, 2024, en route to our first-ever final in the competition. The vastly experienced stopper – who played for Arsenal, ASJ Soyaux in France, Birmingham City, Chelsea and West Ham before signing for Spurs in 2019 – started 21 WSL and cup games in Lilywhite in 2023/24. Capped by England at Under-19 and Under-20 levels, Becky switched her allegiance to Jamaica – qualifying through her heritage – and kept a clean sheet on her senior debut against Nigeria in June, 2021.

ELEANOR HEEPS

Goalkeeper Eleanor signed a new contract with Spurs Women in April, 2024, which will keep her at the Club until the summer of 2027. Joining us after five years in the Liverpool academy, the former England Under-19 international stopper has since gained first team experience in loan spells at Blackburn Rovers, Coventry United and Sheffield United.

ELLA MORRIS

NEW SIGNING

Ella became our second signing of the summer 2024 transfer window, as she arrived on a three-year deal following the expiration of her contract with Southampton. The England youth international, who originally joined Saints when she was 14, was promoted to their first team in 2018/19 while she was named Southampton's Women's Player of the Season and Players' Player of the Season the following term. Ella helped Saints gain promotion from Southern Region Women's Football League at the fifth tier of the Women's football pyramid to the second-tier FA Women's Championship during her time with the club.

AMANDA NILDÉN

After joining Spurs Women on a six-month loan from Juventus in January, 2004, Amanda made the move a permanent one in June, 2024. The attack-minded full-back became a key player for the Lilywhites during the second half of 2023/24, starting ten consecutive games in the WSL and making 16 appearances in all competitions in total, including our FA Cup Final match against Manchester United. At international level, she has made nine appearances for Sweden at the time of writing, and was part of the squad to reach the semi-finals at UEFA Women's Euro 2022.

AMY JAMES-TURNER

Experienced defender Amy had played more than 50 times for Spurs Women by the close of the 2023/24 campaign. She joined the club in the summer of 2022 after a season at Orlando Pride. Before that, Amy had been on the books at Manchester United between 2018 and 2021 and has also turned out for Doncaster Rovers Belles, Leeds United and Liverpool during her career. Born in Sheffield, Amy was capped four times by England in 2015.

MOLLY BARTRIP

A consistent performer for Spurs Women once again in 2023/24, Molly missed just four of our 22 WSL matches during the campaign. The defender joined our Women's first team in July, 2021, years after playing for Spurs' Under-10s! Prior to her return to N17, Molly played more than a hundred games for fellow WSL side Reading.

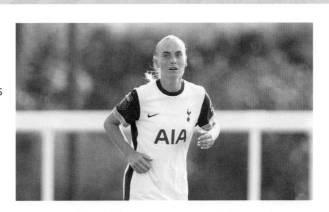

CHARLOTTE GRANT

Full-back Charlotte made 14 appearances and scored once in all competitions for Spurs Women in the second half of 2023/24, after signing for the club in the January transfer window. She has previously played for Swedish sides Rosengård and Vittsjö GIK and her hometown club Adelaide United. Charlotte represents Australia at international level, making her debut in 2021 and she scored her first goal for the Matildas in a 2-0 win over the Lionesses in London in April, 2023.

CLARE HUNT

Clare joined us from Paris Saint-Germain in August, 2024, shortly after featuring in all three of Australia's matches at that summer's Olympic Games. Born in Grenfell, Australia on 12 March, 1999, the defender's career began at Canberra United, for whom she debuted in November, 2016. She moved to Western Sydney Wanderers in 2021 before joining PSG two years later. Her senior international debut came against Czechia in February, 2023.

ASHLEIGH NEVILLE

Our longest-serving player, Ashleigh's start in our 1-0 WSL victory at Bristol City in March, 2024 was her 150th competitive Club appearance. In what was her seventh season in a Spurs shirt, having arrived from Coventry United in 2017, Ashleigh featured in 25 matches for us in 2023/24. Her one and only goal of the campaign came in our 4-2 win at Aston Villa in October, 2023.

LUANA BÜHLER

Luana had a strong finish to her debut season in N17, starting her eighth consecutive game in our last WSL fixture of the campaign at Tottenham Hotspur Stadium where we beat West Ham United 3-1. The Switzerland international made 21 appearances in total during the campaign after joining from 1899 Hoffenheim where she captained the side and played more than a hundred games. She has more than 50 caps for Switzerland and was included in their squads for the Euro 2025 qualifying games, leading the side and scoring in a 4-0 win over Azerbaijan in April, 2024.

OLGA AHTINEN

Finland international Olga played 20 times and scored once during her debut campaign with Spurs in 2023/24. She joined the club in August, 2023 from Swedish top-flight side Linköpings FC, where she was named Most Valuable Player in 2022. Olga had made 61 appearances for Finland prior to the run of Euro 2025 qualifying group games between April and July, 2024, and was part of her country's squad for the 2023 Women's World Cup.

DREW SPENCE

Drew scored twice in 15 appearances for us in 2023/24, having moved across London from Chelsea in June, 2022. The second of those – a powerful strike from 20 yards out against West Ham in the season finale – was nominated for the WSL's Goal of the Season, but she lost out to an effort from Aston Villa's Danielle Turner. The experienced midfielder featured for Jamaica at the 2023 FIFA World Cup as they reached the round of 16.

ARAYA DENNIS

A former Arsenal youth player, Araya signed a professional contract with us in February, 2024. She spent the 2023/24 campaign with Crystal Palace, netting twice in 20 league games in the South Londoners' Barclays Women's Championship-winning campaign. Araya represented England at the 2023 UEFA Women's Under-17 European Championship and played two matches at the 2024 UEFA Women's Under-19 European Championship, where the Young Lionesses reached the semi-finals of both tournaments.

EVELIINA SUMMANEN

Midfielder Eveliina started in all but two of our WSL games in 2023/24 and also played every match in our run to the final of the Women's FA Cup. She has been an important player in the centre of the park for us since signing for the Club in January, 2022 from Swedish side Kristianstad. A Finland international, Eveliina had made 61 appearances for her country prior to the Euro 2025 qualifying group games between April and July, 2024.

SHUANG WANG

A China international with over 100 caps to her name, Shuang joined us in January, 2024 following the expiry of her contract with NWSL club Racing Louisville. The experienced midfielder, formerly of Paris Saint-Germain, made 10 appearances for us in the second half of the 2023/24 season with her debut coming in our WSL match against Manchester City in January, 2024. The AFC Women's Footballer of the Year in 2018, Shuang is also is a four-time Chinese Women's Footballer of the Year.

HAYLEY RASO

An experienced campaigner with over 250 senior appearances to her name, Hayley put pen-to-paper on a two-year contract with us in September 2024. Born in Gold Coast, Queensland, Australia on 5 September, 1994, the attack-minded player began her career with Canberra United and later represented Brisbane Roar (three spells), Washington Spirit, Melbourne Victory (loan) and Portland Thorns before joining Barclays WSL side Everton in 2020. She moved to Manchester City a year later and to Real Madrid in 2023.

JESSICA NAZ

Jessica had a fantastic season in 2023/24, topping Spurs Women's appearances chart and netting seven times in all competitions. The forward's performances also earned her a first call-up to the full England senior squad for two Euro 2025 qualifiers against France in June, 2024. Another player who featured for Spurs as a child, Jess returned to the Club in 2018 from local rivals Arsenal.

ROSELLA AYANE

Rosella made her 100th appearance for Spurs Women in 2023/24 in what was her fifth campaign with the Club having joined from Bristol City in 2019. The milestone match came in March, 2024 as she was substituted on in our 1-0 WSL victory over LeicesterCity. She scored three goals during the campaign, including a 96th-minute winner to complete a 3-2 comeback over Sheffield United in the fourth round of our historic Women's FA Cup run. Having represented England at youth level, Rosella plays for Morocco at senior international level.

MATILDA VINBERG

Midfielder Matilda joined Spurs Women midway through the 2023/24 season following a stint with Hammarby IF. By the end of the campaign, she had made 18 appearances in all competitions for us, and netted once. Having risen through the age groups on the international scene, Matilda made her senior debut for Sweden in November, 2022, and at the time of writing has six caps to her name.

BETHANY ENGLAND

Our Women's Club captain missed the first three months of the 2023/24 WSL season following a hip operation, but hit the pitch running upon her return. Bethany netted eight times in total during the campaign, including a last-gasp equaliser against Manchester City to take our Women's FA Cup quarter-final to a penalty shootout – which we subsequently won. A January, 2023 signing from Chelsea, Bethany's impressive 13 strikes in just 14 appearances in 2022/23, saw her selected to represent the Lionesses at the 2023 FIFA Women's World Cup.

MARTHA THOMAS

Martha made history in 2023/24 as her 58th-minute strike against Arsenal in December 2023 gave us our first-ever win over the Gunners in the WSL. It also won her the Club's Goal of the Season award and she topped our goalscoring charts for the campaign too with 10 strikes in 27 games. Voted the WSL's Player of the Month for October, 2023 after netting a hat-trick for the Lilywhites against Aston Villa, the forward's impressive goalscoring form continued on the international scene as she netted four for Scotland in a 5-0 win over Israel in a Euro 2025 qualifier in June, 2024.

KIT GRAHAM

One of our longest serving players, Kit had made just shy of 90 appearances for Spurs Women by the end of the 2023/24 season. The forward joined the Lilywhites from Charlton Athletic in August, 2019 and was part of our first-ever squad to compete in the WSL. She put pen-to-paper on a new contract in February, 2024 that will keep her at the Club until June, 2025.

LENNA GUNNING-WILLIAMS

Lenna originally joined our under-16 team before progressing through the ranks to sign her first professional contract with us in July 2023. Her initial First Team involvement came when she joined our pre-season tour of Louisville in the summer of 2022 while her First Team debut – and first goal - came in a 5-1 win against Coventry United in the FA Women's Continental Tyres League Cup in November 2022. Lenna scored 14 goals in 26 appearances for Women's National League Southern Premier Division side Ipswich Town whilst on loan during the 2023/24 season.

PLAYER OF THE YEAR AWARDS 2024

In his debut season as a Spurs player, Micky van de Ven completed a clean sweep of the Club's Men's Player of the Season awards in 2023/24.

The Dutchman was named Player of the Season by our Official Supporters' Clubs (OSC) as well as Player of the Season by both One Hotspur Members and One Hotspur Juniors.

He received his One Hotspur awards ahead of our penultimate home match of the 2023/24 Premier League season against Burnley and, fittingly, celebrated by scoring a late winner in front of the adoring South Stand!

Having joined us from Bundesliga side VfL Wolfsburg in the summer of 2023, Micky scored three times in 29 appearances in all competitions in his first season as a Spurs player. But for a serious hamstring injury sustained against Chelsea on 6 November, 2023, which ruled him out for over two months, he surely would have played even more matches. He was included in the Netherlands squad for UEFA Euro 2024.

Grace Clinton, who spent the 2023/24 season on loan with us from Manchester United, also completeda clean sweep of the Women's Player of the Season awards for the campaign. The attack-minded midfielder collected the Supporters' and Junior Supporters' Player of the Season awards as well as the Proud Lilywhites Player of the Season. Her trio of prizes were presented to her after our final FA WSL home match of the season against West Ham United, which was staged at Tottenham Hotspur Stadium.

Martha Thomas was also presented with an award having won Goal of the Season for her historic strike against Arsenal, which brought us a first WSL victory over our local rivals.

DESTINATION TOTTENHAM

TOTTENHAM HOTSPUR STADIUM

FOUR EXCITING ATTRACTIONS, ONE ICONIC STADIUM

SPURS IN

78,000 fans turned out for our post-season clash with Newcastle United at Australia's famous Melbourne Cricket Ground on 22 May, 2024.

The fixture – which saw Ange Postecoglou return to his homeland – saw some of our younger players take to the pitch, with Alfie Devine, Ashley Phillips, George Abbott, Jamie Donley, Dane Scarlett, Yago Santiago, Tyrese Hall, Rio Kyerematen and Leo Black all gaining valuable game time.

James Maddison fired Spurs into the lead on 32 minutes after he intercepted a pass from Magpies 'keeper Nick Pope that was meant for Miguel Almiron, and our number 10 rifled the ball into the back of the net from eight yards out.

Just before half-time, Alexander Isak tapped home from close range after Brandon Austin parried a shot from Jacob Murphy, to make it 1-1.

AUSTRALIA

We dominated the game and had chances late on to win it but Emerson Royal glanced Bryan Gil's corner past the post and Donley hit a low shot just wide from 20 yards out. With no further goals in the second half, the friendly match went to penalties.

Gil saw his effort saved by Newcastle's substitute goalkeeper Mark Gillespie, so even though Scarlett, Donley, Hall and Oliver Skipp all converted thereafter, the Magpies scored all five of their spot-kicks to give our Premier League rivals a 5-4 shootout victory.

Spurs Line-up: Austin (Whiteman 78), Porro (Abbott 46 (Black 88)), Dragusin (Hall 71), Van de Ven (Phillips 46), Royal (Kyerematen 88), Bentancur (Skipp 46), Sarr (Donley 61), Maddison (Devine 46), Johnson (Santiago 69), Kulusevski (Scarlett 69), Son (Bryan 61)

HEART OF MIDLOTHIAN 1 SPURS 5

Tynecastle Stadium, Edinburgh | 17 July, 2024

Pre-season got off to the perfect start as we beat Heart of Midlothian 5-1 in Edinburgh in a match held as part of the Scottish side's 150th anniversary celebrations. New arrivals Archie Gray and Lucas Bergvall made their first appearances in our colours as a total of 25 of our players were given minutes during the match.

Brennan Johnson opened the scoring for us just before the break, but Lawrence Shankland equalised for the home side straight after the interval. From then on it was all Spurs though. Will Lankshear – top scorer in our title-winning Under-21 team last season – restored our lead before 16-year-old Mikey Moore made it 3-1.

Djed Spence tapped home from close range for Spurs' fourth and we completed our rout five minutes from time when Ashley Phillips bundled a loose ball over the line at the back post.

VISSEL KOBE 2 SPURS 3

National Stadium, Tokyo | 27 July, 2024

Spurs came from behind to beat Vissel Kobe 3-2 at Japan's National Stadium in the first match of our pre-season tour to Asia. Pedro Porro cancelled out Yuya Osaka's opener for the J League champions when Dejan Kulusevski flicked the ball into his path and he slid it home on 17 minutes.

Son and Johnson combined shortly after the restart as our captain made it 2-1, but the home side – 24 games into their domestic campaign - drew level just after the hour mark in front of a 54,000-strong crowd.

Four minutes from time, youngster Jamie Donley crossed from the left byline for his fellow Academy team mate Moore to tap home his second goal of pre-season.

QUEENS PARK RANGERS 0 SPURS 2

Loftus Road, London | 20 July, 2024

Yves Bissouma and Dane Scarlett were on target for Spurs against QPR to make it two pre-season wins out of two. With almost 30 minutes on the clock at Loftus Road, Heung-Min Son had a good chance for us before Brandon Austin tipped Rayan Kolli's long-range effort onto the crossbar at the other end.

Rangers had the ball in the net first but Michael Frey was ruled offside and shortly after, Bissouma produced some dazzling footwork to slot home the opener – and his first goal in our colours – just before half-time.

Ange Postecoglou made ten changes at half-time and Rangers started to ramp up the pressure in the second half. They came closest to an equaliser in the 86th minute, but Spurs substitute goalkeeper Luca Gunter pulled off a flying save to tip Lyndon Dykes' header onto the post. Seconds later at the other end, Scarlett converted Moore's cross to make the game safe.

TEAM K LEAGUE 3 SPURS 4
Seoul World Cup Stadium, Seoul | 31 July, 2024

Our summer tour continued in Korea, with fans treated to a seven-goal thriller against Team K League at the Seoul World Cup Stadium.

Spurs raced into a 3-0 half-time lead as Kulusevski pounced on a rebound and lifted the ball into the roof of the net from six yards out, and Son – back on home soil – bagged a brace, with the first of those a stunning curling strike into the top corner after a fine pass in to him from Donley.

The local all-star side – who featured our new signing Yang Min-Hyeok in their line-up – pulled it back to 3-2 early in the second half. Lankshear struck our fourth before Team K League responded through Oberdan with nine minutes remaining, but we held on for our fourth straight win in pre-season.

BAYERN MUNICH 2 SPURS 1
Seoul World Cup Stadium, Seoul | 3 August, 2024

Bayern Munich inflicted our first defeat of pre-season as our summer tour ended with a 2-1 loss in Seoul. The German outfit – under new manager Vincent Kompany but without former Spur Harry Kane in the line-up – took the lead through Gabriel Vidovic after just four minutes and they continued to dominate throughout the first half.

Both sides made a number of substitutions from half-time onwards, with the familiar face of another ex-Lilywhite, Eric Dier, introduced from the bench for Bayern. Spurs had the first opening of the second period when Kulusevski drilled a shot inches wide but Leon Goretzka doubled Bayern's advantage shortly before the hour mark.

We worked our way back into the game thanks to one of Porro's trademark thunderbolts on 66 minutes and it was almost 2-2 moments later too, Porro's fine pass finding Bergvall on the edge of the area but he fired wide with just the goalkeeper to beat and the score remained unchanged.

SPURS 2 BAYERN MUNICH 3
Tottenham Hotspur Stadium | 10 August, 2024

Our two former stars, Kane and Dier, received a warm welcome on their return to a packed-out Tottenham Hotspur Stadium, as Spurs went down to a second narrow defeat in seven days against Bayern.

We went in front after just 23 seconds of the Visit Malta Cup match when Kulusevski finished from six yards out after a fine run down the right and cross into the area by Johnson. The Germans responded quickly and goals from Dayot Upamecano, Serge Gnabry and Thomas Muller saw them go in 3-1 up at the break.

Kulu netted his third goal of pre-season just after the hour mark to reduce the deficit but we were unable to find the equaliser. Kane, who came on with 12 minutes remaining and was greeted with rapturous applause, twice went close in the final minutes but fired over on each occasion.

WORDSEARCH

Can you find the surnames of EIGHT members of our Women's squad?
ANSWERS ON PAGES 60-61

B	A	H	T	I	N	E	N	A	J
D	L	C	S	A	M	O	H	T	K
B	K	E	N	G	L	A	N	D	V
G	A	G	T	O	I	N	E	E	S
R	A	R	A	X	L	N	V	R	P
E	A	A	T	N	L	E	I	L	E
B	R	N	E	R	E	S	L	E	N
N	F	T	T	L	I	T	L	C	C
I	A	L	U	R	G	P	E	H	E
V	D	B	A	A	E	L	F	T	R

AHTINEN   NEVILLE
BARTRIP   SPENCER
ENGLAND   THOMAS
GRANT   VINBERG

LEGENDS CROSSWORD

DOWN

1. Scored for us in both the 1962 FA Cup Final and the 1963 European Cup Winners' Cup Final (two goals). Jimmy _ _ _ _ _ _ _ (7)

2. Welsh winger who returned to us on loan in 2020/21 after a successful first spell with the club between 2007 and 2013. Gareth _ _ _ _ (4)

3. Ex-Spur who played for Belgium at UEFA Euro 2024. Jan _ _ _ _ _ _ _ _ _ _ (10)

4. Ex-England striker who now hosts Match of the Day. Gary _ _ _ _ _ _ _ (7)

6. The Republic of Ireland's most capped player and record goalscorer, who spent two spells with us between 2002 and 2011. Robbie _ _ _ _ _ (5)

9. German striker who signed for us in 1994 and 1997. Jurgen _ _ _ _ _ _ _ _ _ (9)

ACROSS

5. Our former captain who skippered France to World Cup glory in 2018. Hugo _ _ _ _ _ _ (6)

7. Striker who returned to the Club in 2022 as an ambassador and academy coach. Jermain _ _ _ _ _ (5)

8. Former England midfielder nicknamed 'Gazza'. Paul _ _ _ _ _ _ _ _ _ (9)

10. Captain of our 1960/61 'Double' winning team. Danny _ _ _ _ _ _ _ _ _ _ _ _ (12)

11. Our all-time record goalscorer. Harry _ _ _ _ (4)

SPOT THE DIFFERENCE

Spot the SIX differences in these two team photographs of Spurs Women prior to the 2024 Adobe FA Cup Final… ANSWERS ON PAGES 60-61

WHO ARE YA?

Guess our 2024/25 Premier League opponents from the following emojis...
ANSWERS ON PAGES 60-61

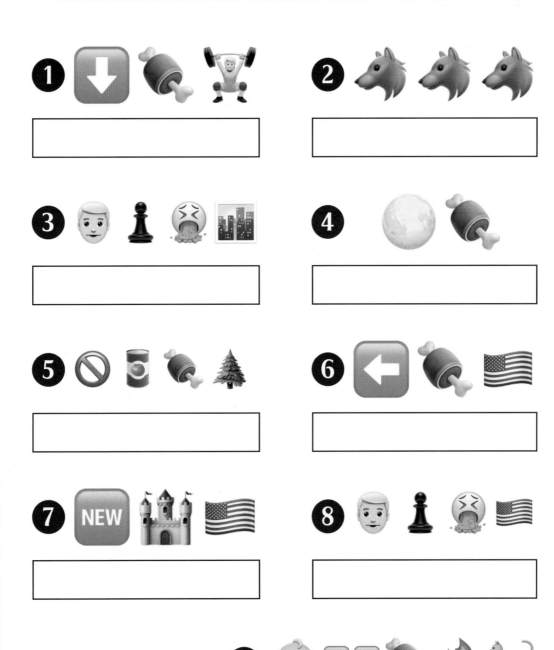

1

2

3

4

5

6

7

8

AND WHICH PREMIER LEAGUE CLUB IS THIS?...

9

LEGACY

N U M B E R S

You might notice a small number that appears above the player's name on the back of our Men's first team shirt. Do you know what that number is? The answer is, a 'legacy number'.

During the 2023/24 season, after an extensive research project, we became the first professional football club in England to assign a unique legacy number to every player in our rich and illustrious history that has made a senior competitive appearance for Tottenham Hotspur… over 880 players and counting! As you will have seen, legacy numbers do not replace the larger squad numbers that continue to be worn on the back of match shirts.

An FA Cup tie with West Herts on 13 October, 1894 is our first recorded senior competitive fixture, with the starting XI that day assigned numbers 1-11 in alphabetical order – Stanley Briggs (#1), Archie Cubberley (#2), James Eccles (#3), Donald Goodall (#4), Peter Hunter (#5), Bill Julian (#6), Jack Jull (#7), Cuthbert Monk (#8), Ernie Payne (#9), Jack Shepherd (#10) and Jack Welham (#11).

Spanning every competitive match from that 1894 FA Cup tie to date, our legacy number list includes every individual from single appearance makers to Steve Perryman (#477), who has played more matches for Tottenham Hotspur (854) than anyone else. These are some of the other legendary players you can find on the list…

#420

DANNY BLANCHFLOWER

Danny Blanchflower left an indelible mark on the Club in a trophy-laden decade in north London. One of the finest players to ever pull on our Lilywhite shirt, the Northern Irishman was the inspirational captain behind our iconic 1960/61 'Double'-winning side, while also leading us to another FA Cup in 1962 and the European Cup Winners' Cup the following season.

#498

GLENN HODDLE

#448

JIMMY GREAVES

Goalscorer supreme Jimmy Greaves netted 266 times in 381 matches. Up until Harry Kane broke his Club record in 2023, 'Greavsie' had long topped our scoring charts. Notable goals from him included a hat-trick on his Spurs debut against Blackpool in December, 1961, a strike in our 3-1 victory over Burnley in the 1962 FA Cup Final and a brace as we beat Atlético Madrid 5-1 in the 1963 European Cup Winners' Cup Final.

A pure footballing genius, Glenn Hoddle netted 110 times in 490 appearances for us between 1975 and 1987. Renowned for his vision and range of passing, the midfielder was also the scorer of some great goals. These included acrobatic volleys against Nottingham Forest and Manchester United at White Hart Lane in 1979, a delightful turn and chip against Watford in 1983 and a wonderful solo effort in his penultimate home match for us against Oxford United in 1987. He starred in our FA Cup Final victory over Manchester City in 1981 alongside World Cup winners Ossie Ardiles (#511) and Ricky Villa (#513) and won the cup again with us a year later.

The legacy numbers of other Club goalscoring greats include

#426 Bobby Smith   **#599** Teddy Sheringham
#434 Cliff Jones   **#617** Jürgen Klinsmann
#458 Alan Gilzean   **#672** Robbie Keane
#469 Martin Chivers   **#686** Jermain Defoe
#580 Gary Lineker

#573

PAUL GASCOIGNE

Paul Gascoigne spearheaded our run to the 1991 FA Cup Final with six goals in five matches en route to the showpiece occasion. Amongst those goals was a memorable free-kick against Arsenal in the semi-final at Wembley, in which current Match of the Day presenter Gary Lineker (#580) also scored twice in a 3-1 Spurs win. Sadly Gazza sustained a serious injury playing in the 1991 FA Cup Final victory over Nottingham Forest, in what would prove to be his final appearance in our colours after scoring 33 goals in 112 appearances.

#649

LEDLEY KING

Ledley joined our Youth Academy aged 14 and became a trainee in July, 1996, before going on to become one of the finest defenders the Club has ever seen. He featured in 323 first-team matches for us between 1999 and 2012, scoring 14 goals. But for long-term knee problems, he would surely have played many, many more. Working as an ambassador for the Club these days, along with other great former players such as Gary Mabbutt (#538), Ledley will always be king of N17!

#726

GARETH BALE

'Taxi for Maicon' sang the White Hart Lane faithful, as Gareth Bale produced a virtuoso performance in our 3-1 win over then-European champions Inter Milan in November, 2010. Having scored a hat-trick against the same opponents in the Champions League less than a month earlier, the Welshman had truly announced himself on the world stage. Twice named PFA Player of the Year (2011 and 2013) during his first spell as a Spurs player, when he netted 55 times in 203 matches between 2007 and 2013, Bale later returned for a season-long loan with us in 2020/21. He won 15 trophies during his time at Real Madrid, including five Champions Leagues.

#781

HUGO LLORIS

Hugo Lloris became the first Spurs player to captain a World Cup-winning team, as he lifted the trophy aloft following France's 4-2 victory over Croatia in Moscow in the final of 15 July, 2018. The Nice-born goalkeeper has made more Premier League appearances for us and kept more clean sheets than any other player. He wore our colours 361 times in the division and produced 127 shut-outs between 2012 and 2024. Hugo is one of a number of goalkeeping greats to have played for us.

Honourable mentions also have to go to

#364 Ted Ditchburn   **#578** Erik Thorstvedt
#440 Bill Brown   **#589** Ian Walker
#455 Pat Jennings   **#693** Paul Robinson
#523 Ray Clemence   **#876** Guglielmo Vicario

#787

HARRY KANE

Our greatest-ever goalscorer, Harry Kane became one of the world's best players in his time in north London. An Academy graduate, Harry enjoyed quite the journey with us and went on to take Jimmy Greaves' all-time goalscoring record (266) for the Club in his final season in N17, scoring a staggering 280 goals in Lilywhite

#805

HEUNG-MIN SON

Sonny, whose player profile can be found elsewhere in this annual, captained the first Spurs team to wear legacy numbers during our 2-1 win at Crystal Palace in October, 2023. The team that night, with their legacy numbers listed was:

#876 Vicario   **#868** Sarr   (**#861** Bentancur)
#870 Porro   **#864** Bissouma   **#865** Richarlison
#853 Romero   (**#841** Højbjerg)   (**#878** Johnson)
#875 Van de Ven   **#860** Kulusevski   **#805** Son
#796 Davies   (**#854** Gil)
(**#858** Royal)   **#873** Maddison

LIVE AND DIRECT!

Rapper, singer, songwriter and record producer AJ Tracey rose to national prominence back in 2015 as tracks from his second EP Alex Moran started being platformed by radio stations including BBC Radio 1Xtra. Now one of the biggest grime/rap acts in the UK, 2024 saw the release of his third studio album (untitled at the time of writing). His previous two albums, AJ Tracey and Flu Game, both charted in the UK's top three.

While AJ was born and raised in west London, he has strong connections to N17 with his Spurs-supporting dad a former resident of Broadwater Farm. A season ticket holder himself, AJ's longstanding relationship with Spurs saw his hit single False 9 provide the soundtrack to our Nike kit release in the summer of 2017, as he starred in our kit promotion that year. In 2022, fresh from his debut at Glastonbury, he flew to Seoul to watch our tour matches against Team K League and Sevilla in the Coupang Play Series and even took part in an open training session at Mokdong Stadium!

Ahead of the start of the 2024/25 season, we spoke to AJ about his music career, love for Spurs and also got him to name a 'Spurs Dream XI', based on his favourite players over the years…

HI AJ. FIRSTLY, CAN YOU TELL US HOW YOU BECAME A SPURS SUPPORTER?

My dad's from Tottenham. When I was a baby, he stuck me in a Spurs shirt and that was it. I think it was a rite of passage. My first Spurs shirt was a purple PONY shirt. I've still got that shirt. It's tiny, but I'll never get rid of it.

I can't remember the year I first went to White Hart Lane to see my first match but I went with my dad and my little brother. I reckon it was about 18 years ago.

WHAT HAVE BEEN YOUR HIGHLIGHTS SUPPORTING SPURS OVER THE YEARS?

I loved the team under Poch (Mauricio Pochettino) and I love Ange's team right now. One of the obvious highlights was our run in the Champions League (in 2018/19), that led to that semi-final against Ajax and the final against Liverpool. It's a shame that we didn't get it over the line by winning the final… I think fate was slightly against us that night and it pains me every time I see that clip (of Moussa Sissoko's handball that led to Liverpool being awarded a penalty in the 2019 Champions League Final)! But what a run it was that season… drawing in Barcelona to go through to the knockout phase… beating Borussia Dortmund… the incredible quarter-final against Manchester City and of course Lucas Moura's hat-trick in Amsterdam.

> **66 99**
>
> **Harry Kane's in there. Our all-time record goalscorer and someone who I had the fortune to watch live so many times in my lifetime. That was an absolute privilege.**

WHO HAVE BEEN YOUR FAVOURITE SPURS PLAYERS OVER THE YEARS AND WHY?

There are three that spring to mind. I have lots of favourite Spurs players I never saw play but I have to go with players I watched regularly in the flesh. (Heung-Min) Son is my all-time favourite. I think he embodies Tottenham in the way he plays and he's a nice guy too. I've been lucky to meet him a few times and I admire his fashion sense too!

Gareth Bale. He was unbelievable for us. He must have been an absolute nightmare to play against. We all remember what he did to Maicon in the Champions League. And of course, Harry Kane's in there. Our all-time record goalscorer and someone who I had the fortune to watch live so many times in my lifetime. That was an absolute privilege.

I want to give honourable mentions to Jan Vertonghen and Mousa Dembélé too.

HOW OFTEN DO YOU GET TO SPURS MATCHES?

I've got a season ticket in the East Stand. I barely miss a home game and I try to get to away games when I can too.

HOW DO YOU REFLECT ON THE 2023/24 SEASON AND WHAT ARE YOUR HOPES FOR 2024/25?

We saw progress in 2023/24. It felt like we went into the season at the start of a rebuilding process and I think, finishing fifth, was a good achievement early on in the project. I'd have been happy with that at the start of the season. I had a lot of time for (Antonio) Conte, but the football was a hard watch at times. We were enjoying our football again last season under Ange.

In 2024/25, I just want to see us continue to build. I'm excited for the Europa League. I think we can have a good run in that. And it would be great to get back in the Champions League.

WHAT ARE YOUR THOUGHTS ON ANGE POSTECOGLOU?

I love 'Big Ange'. He speaks really well. With so many clubs having to bring in new managers over the summer (of 2024), I think it's a blessing we've got someone like Ange. He's the sort of manager who will hopefully be here for the long run.

CAN YOU TELL US A BIT ABOUT YOUR INVOLVEMENT WITH THE CLUB OVER THE YEARS?

I am a lifelong Spurs fan and I am so fortunate to have a relationship both with the Club and Nike. It has been great to get involved with things like kit launches in the past. I'm always happy to promote Spurs and it works both ways. The Club have been great, blasting my albums around the stadium on matchdays.

I got to go to Korea one year when Spurs were there. I watched the matches there and I even got to join in with some of the training. That was totally surreal, as I'm sure any Spurs fan would appreciate. I've also got to meet some of the Spurs board members, including Daniel Levy, and there's that real mutual respect there.

I'd say the most rewarding aspect of my relationship with the Club though is with the work they do in the local community. The feeling of knowing I can help make a difference alongside the Club is very rewarding indeed.

AND YOUR LOVE OF SPURS EXTENDS TO BOTH OUR MEN'S AND WOMEN'S TEAMS?

Absolutely. I'm so happy to see the spotlight on women's football in recent years. It has been long overdue. I'm also so proud of what this Spurs Women's team has achieved in a short period of time. Getting to an FA Cup Final last season was sick. What a team we have… we've got some quality players in there and we can only keep on getting better and better in my opinion!

YOU'VE BEEN IN THE MUSIC INDUSTRY FOR AROUND 15 YEARS. CAN YOU TELL US A BIT ABOUT HOW YOU GOT STARTED AND ALSO YOUR CAREER HIGHLIGHTS OVER THE YEARS?

I started making music in my friend's bedroom and I uploaded some things to SoundCloud to see if anyone liked it. I got a really positive response and started doing radio shows and it all took off from there.

In terms of highlights, playing at Glastonbury was incredible with 100,000 people there. It was special. Not to sound too Tottenham-orientated, but I'd have to say having my music played season on season at Spurs on matchdays is genuinely one of the things that has meant most to me on my journey. It's massive.

WHAT'S ON THE HORIZON FOR YOU IN 2025?
I released a new album in the second half of 2024, so 2025 will be a year of touring… more music, more shows…

AJ TRACEY'S DREAM SPURS XI

AJ chose his favourite Spurs XI of all-time in a 4-3-3 formation

HUGO LLORIS

KYLE WALKER

JAN VERTONGHEN

LEDLEY KING

DANNY ROSE

CHRISTIAN ERIKSEN

MOUSA DEMBÉLÉ

LUKA MODRIĆ

HEUNG-MIN SON

HARRY KANE

GARETH BALE

SUPER SPURS QUIZ

Test your knowledge of your favourite club with these 20 questions...
ANSWERS ON PAGES 60-61

1. Who scored our opening goal of the 2023/24 Barclays Women's Super League (WSL) season in a 2-1 defeat at Chelsea in October 2023?

2. What nationality is Spurs Women Head Coach, Robert Vilahamn?

3. Molly Bartrip and which Finnish international were Spurs Women's vice-captain during the 2023/24 season?

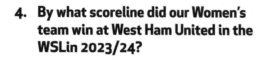

4. By what scoreline did our Women's team win at West Ham United in the WSL in 2023/24?

5. Our run to the 2024 Adobe Women's FA Cup Final began with victory over which FA Women's Championship side in the fourth round?

6. At what ground did we face Leicester City in the 2024 Women's FA Cup semi-final?

7. In which South Yorkshire town was Bethany England born on 3 June, 1994?

8. In which stadium did Spurs Women stage the majority of their home matches in 2023/24?

9. Which London club did we beat in the FA WSL for the first time in 2023?

10. Which Scottish club did our Men's Head Coach Ange Postecoglou used to manage?

11. Which United States international, who has played over 200 matches for her country and scored 100-plus international goals, spent a loan spell with Spurs Women in 2020?

12. With 17 goals in all competitions, who was our Men's top scorer in 2023/24?

13. Which position does Cristian Romero play?

14. What appeared on the back of our Men's player shirts for the first time for our Premier League match at Crystal Palace in October, 2023?

15. Which Premier League club did we face in a post-season friendly in Melbourne, Australia in May, 2024?

16. Which German player spent part of the 2023/24 season on loan with us from RB Leipzig and returned for another loan spell?

17. What nationality is Micky van de Ven?

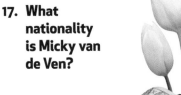

18. Cristian Romero and which other player were appointed as our Men's vice-captains at the start of the 2023/24 season?

19. At which stadium did our Men's team play their first match of the 2024/25 Premier League season?

20. Which German club did our Men's team face in two friendly matches prior to the start of the 2024/25 season?

ANSWERS

WORDSEARCH
P46

B	A	H	T	I	N	E	N	A	J
D	L	C	S	A	M	O	H	T	K
B	K	E	N	G	L	A	N	D	V
G	A	G	T	O	I	N	E	E	S
R	A	R	A	X	L	N	V	R	P
E	A	A	T	N	L	E	I	L	E
B	R	N	E	R	E	S	L	E	N
N	F	T	T	L	I	T	L	C	C
I	A	L	U	R	G	P	E	H	E
V	D	B	A	S	E	L	F	T	R

1. G R E A V E
2. B A L E
3. V E R T O N G E N
4. L I N E K E R
5. L L O R I S
6. K E A N E
7. D E F O E
8. G A S C O I G N E
9. K L I N S M A N N
10. B L A N C H F L O W E R
    H E N
11. K A N E

LEGENDS CROSSWORD
P47

60

ANSWERS

SPOT THE DIFFERENCE P48

WHO ARE YA!?
P49

1. **Southampton**
   (South-Ham-Ton)
2. **Wolves**
3. **Manchester City**
   (Man-Chess-Urgh! City)
4. **Fulham** (Full(Moon)-Ham)
5. **Nottingham Forest**
   (Not-Tin-Ham Forest)
6. **West Ham United**
7. **Newcastle United**
   (New-Castle United)
8. **Manchester United**
   (Man-Chess-Urgh! United)
9. **Tottenham Hotspur**
   (Tot-Ten-Ham Hot-S-Purr)

SUPER SPURS QUIZ
P58-59

1. **Martha Thomas**
2. **Swedish**
3. **Olga Ahtinen**
4. **4-3**
5. **Sheffield United**
6. **Tottenham Hotspur**
   Stadium
7. **Barnsley**
8. **Brisbane Road**
9. **Arsenal**
10. **Celtic**
11. **Alex Morgan**
12. **Heung-Min Son**
13. **Defender**
    (Centre-Back)
14. **Legacy Numbers**
15. **Newcastle United**
16. **Timo Werner**
17. **Dutch**
18. **James Maddison**
19. **King Power**
    Stadium (home of
    Leicester City)
20. **Bayern Munich**

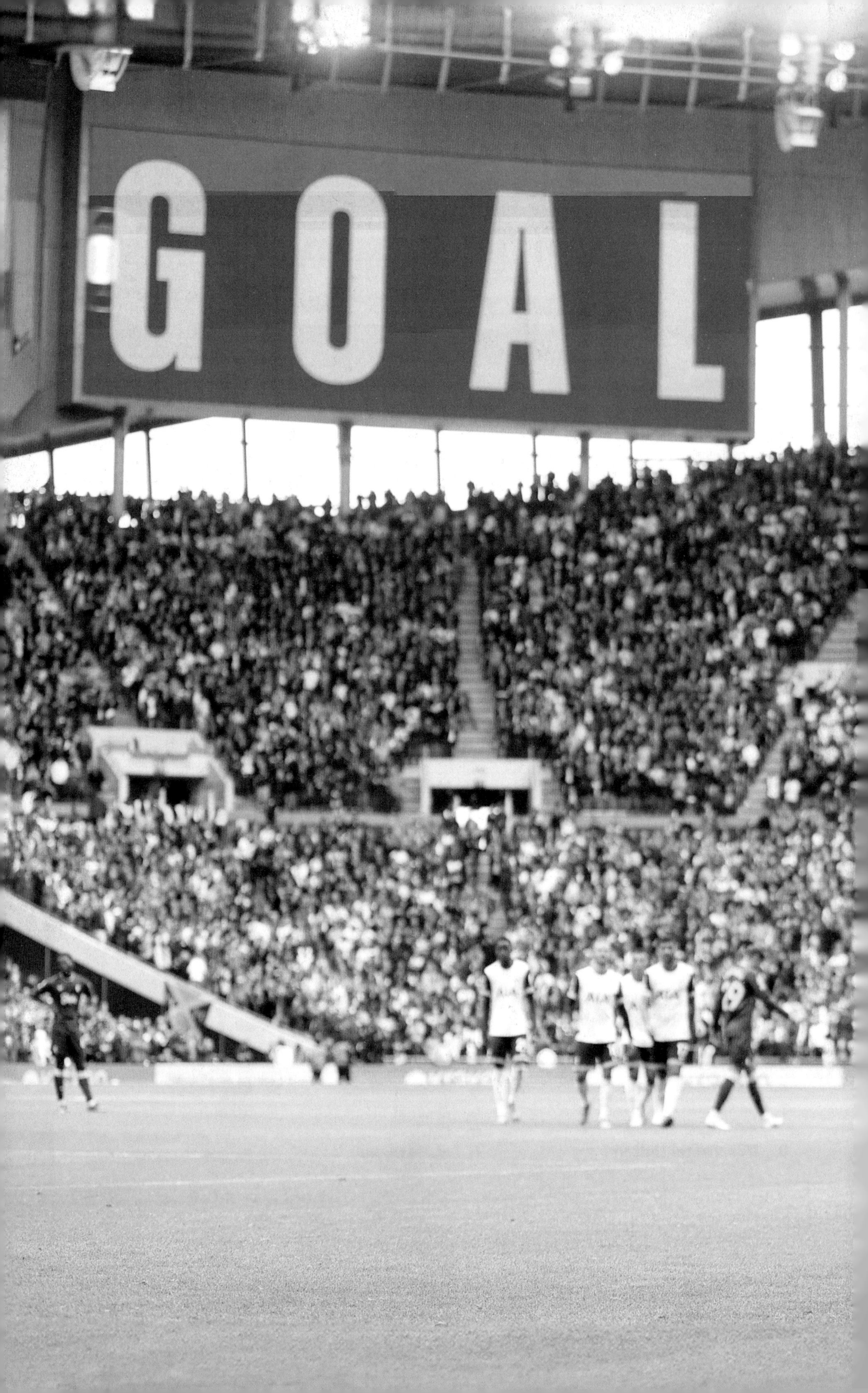
GOAL